A ROOKIE READER ®

MESSY BESSEY

By Patricia and Fredrick McKissack

Illustrations by Richard Hackney

Prepared under the direction of Robert Hillerich, Ph.D.

CHILDRENS PRESS ®

CHICAGO

To Mom Bess
who is **never** *a* *mess*

Library of Congress Cataloging in Publication Data

McKissack, Pat, 1944-
  Messy Bessey.

  (A Rookie Reader)
  Summary: Bessy finally cleans up her messy room.
  [1. Cleanliness—Fiction. 2. Behavior—Fiction]
I. McKissack, Fredrick. II. Hackney, Rick, ill. III. Series.
PZ7.M478693Me   1987   [E]   87-15079
ISBN 0-516-02083-8

Childrens Press®, Chicago
Copyright © 1987 by Regensteiner Publishing Enterprises, Inc.
All rights reserved. Published simultaneously in Canada.
Printed in the United States of America.
1 2 3 4 5 6 7 8 9 10 R 96 95 94 93 92 91 90 89 88 87

Look at your room,
Messy Bessey.

See, colors on the wall,

books on the chair,

toys in the dresser drawer,

and games everywhere.

Messy Bessey, your room
is a mess.

See, shoes on the bed,
coat on the floor,

socks on the table,
and your hat on the door.

Bessey look at your
messy room.

See, the cup in the closet,
cookies on the pillow,

gum on the ceiling,
and jam on the door.

Messy, Messy Bessey,
your room is a mess.

Get the soap and water.

Get the mop and broom.

Get busy Messy Bessey,
you must clean your room.

19

20

So, Bessey rubbed and
scrubbed the walls,

the ceiling,

and the floor.

j39165

She made her bed,

picked up her things,

and closed the closet door.

Hurrah! Good for you
Miss Bessey.
Just look at you, too.

Your room is clean
and beautiful . . .

just like you!

WORD
LIST

		is	see
a	cookies	jam	she
and	cup	just	shoes
at	door	like	so
beautiful	drawer	look	soap
bed	dresser	made	socks
Bessey	everywhere	mess(y)	table
books	floor	Messy	the
broom	for	Miss	things
busy	games	mop	too
ceiling	get	must	toys
chair	good	on	up
clean	gum	picked	wall
closed	hat	pillow	walls
closet	her	room	water
coat	hurrah	rubbed	you
colors	in	scrubbed	your

About the Authors

Patricia and **Fredrick McKissack** are freelance writers, editors, and teachers of writing. They are the owners of All-Writing Services, located in Clayton, Missouri. Since 1975, the McKissacks have published numerous magazine articles and stories for juvenile and adult readers. They also have conducted educational and editorial workshops throughout the country. The McKissacks and their three teenage sons live in a large remodeled inner-city home in St. Louis.

About the Artist

Richard Hackney is a San Francisco illustrator and writer who graduated from Art Center School in Los Angeles, California. He has worked at Disney Studios, drawn a syndicated comic strip, and has been an art director in advertising. He has also done some acting, written children's stories, and currently is doing a lot of educational illustration.

Richard lives with his wife, Elizabeth, and a black cat in a home on the edge of San Francisco Bay.